William Cushing Bamburgh

# Giacomo

A Venetian Tale

William Cushing Bamburgh

**Giacomo**
*A Venetian Tale*

ISBN/EAN: 9783337246570

Printed in Europe, USA, Canada, Australia, Japan

Cover: Foto ©Andreas Hilbeck / pixelio.de

More available books at **www.hansebooks.com**

# GIACOMO:

# A VENETIAN TALE

# Giacomo: A Venetian Tale

By
WILLIAM
CUSHING
BAMBURGH

NEW YORK CITY:

PRIVATELY PRINTED FOR THE AUTHOR

MDCCCXCII

GIOVANNI, - A VENETIAN DUKE
ROSALBA, - - HIS WIFE
PAOLA, - THEIR DAUGHTER
GIACOMO, - A VENETIAN YOUTH

SCENE THE FIRST,
ON THE LIDO.

SCENE THE SECOND,
IN GIOVANNI'S PALACE.

# SCENE THE FIRST

## I.

### GIOVANNI.

Thou say'st 't was done in love?

### GIACOMO.

           Aye, so 't was done;
Nor is it meet that thus my lowly pride
In sweet remembrance of the deed I did
Should leave me still unconscious of my love.
My hope is hope for thee, nor should my love
E'er crave return of all I gave for thee:
Thou art my dream: on thee no sun has set
That I've not yearned should soon again arise,
That on thy peaceful countenance mine eyes
Might linger thro' an hour ere it then
Should set.

### PAOLA.

    Who art thou that to me shouldst thus
Rehearse thy love?  What gratitude must I
Owe unto one on whom no eye of mine
Has beamed as thou dost boldly say it beamed?
O Father, know you he a stranger is,
Who in some uncouth gondola hath passed

And peered into mine eyes when in a dream
I gazed up into Heaven and wondered whence
Our spirits go in death.

GIOVANNI.

                Nay, fret not so,
His story is but one of many; yet,
It is my will that thou shouldst grant him
     court—
And with thy Mother—not so young as thou
Art now at her same age, for care had fall'n
More deeply, tho' the heart that now beats
     time
With this in mine own breast, is still as true
And full of youth as then when flighty youths
And many sleek young beaus were set to win
The tender maid that I, a stranger, held
Within my heart more precious than my name
Which still a most unsullied passport is
Where'er that name is known.

GIACOMO.

                I know it not.

GIOVANNI.

Nor shalt until to-night. 'T is well some men
Assail the birth of men more nobly born,

For they have nought but chance of lowly
  birth
And all the weight that flighty fortune bears :
Respect is none the less from god to god
Than man to man,—of Heaven it is a part :
For one that doth but raise an eye in scorn
Of true respect, doth lose the fragrance sweet
Of gentle manhood.  Giac'mo, come this night,
And if thine oar but splash thy thigh, thy tale
Will fill thy brain and burst ere it be told.—
Farewell.

PAOLA.

  Farewell.

GIACOMO.

     A mortal still am I ;
To-night, in thy sweet presence I will feel
A god.  (*Exeunt Paola and Giovanni.*]
  And ye, O Muses, from thy peak
Of far-away Parnassus, o'er my tongue
Hold sway, lest fate should cut the thread
  and lose
Me this sweet prize.  Farewell, O Paola sweet,
Thou hast upon my heart cast such a spell,
I'm thine and only thine. Farewell ! Farewell !

# SCENE THE SECOND

## II.

### ROSALBA.

'T was but a month ago I saw this youth,
Methinks, slow pass us resting on his oar.
He scanned our faces as one doth look
For some lost jewel in a dingy room.

### PAOLA.

Aye, Mother; and his look did tantalize
For I did look away, and still his face
Enlightened was with so much satisfaction
I fain did look again and penetrate
His sweet and open countenance whereon
No foolish madness seeméd e'er could brood.

### GIOVANNI.

" O Father, know you he a stranger is
Who in some uncouth gondola hath passed
And looked into mine eyes—"

### PAOLA.

      Nay, Father; cease,
And mock me not; 'twas so I spake when he

Before me stood.—'Tis woman's way to build
A barricade of fibs for man to climb
Into the recess of a woman's heart;—
'Tis well that here he comes!

*Enter Giacomo.*

### GIACOMO.

Sweet grace be thine!

### ROSALBA.

And thine, good youth!    How luminous those
      eyes!
'Tis strange, Giovanni, that in that noble face
I see resemblance unto yours when youth
Began to crown the life that's with mine blent.

### GIOVANNI.

To me?

### ROSALBA.

To thee.

### GIOVANNI.

What folly!    Youth begin
And let no falt'ring thought trip up thy speech.

GIACOMO.

Torcello saw my birth—

GIOVANNI.

Torcello?

GIACOMO.

Aye!

PAOLA.

Why, Father; you do wince as if that name
Were part of thy great title.

GIOVANNI.

Silent be,
And listen to this tale.   I hold belief
That ere this night awakes, the dead will rise
In such a strange, unholy fashion, we
Will love our guest.   Proceed then, with thy
        tale.

GIACOMO.

I would not have thee think me but a count
Of fair Torcello!   Soon my parents went
To Giudecca, where was born a girl
Upon whose joy I lived.   In her sweet life

I sunk my life; for her I lived, and since
Her loss, I've wandered beggarlike abroad
With all the taunts uncivil and untrue
That now beset Capuchin friars that roam
From that once pleasant island and become
Low grasping beggars: they deserve the curse
Of Pope or prelate: so at me were cast
Coarse taunts.    That sister's saintlike visage,
        blent
With memory, guided all my prayers; to her
I made confession; until now, my love
Hath sculptured in my breast an holy shrine
Wherein her eyes so saintlike and so pure
Do counsel me.   My precept she became—
To her I vowed my love should be so true
That mingled with a lover's love with mine
A brother's love should make it doubly shine.


### GIOVANNI.

Thou dost begin so well I do bestow
Much praise.

### PAOLA.

        Hold, Father; you do interrupt;—
A shame it is his speech should thus be maimed.

## GIACOMO.

At San Lazarro was I schooled ; in art
'T was Tintoretto I did emulate,
For in the East, Palladio's church doth stand
A sentinel o'er the Lido and the isles
That seem to float upon the river tides
Which heave and fall as doth a mother's breast,
But as perfume doth leave the zephyr sweet
So art did from my life evaporate :
No teacher schooled me, but the spirit came
And ebbed and all I learnt I either saw
Or felt with all the cruelty of a life
Well blest in laziness and in hunger's wit.
In wild seclusion the Euganian Hills
Have sheltered me, and gazing up to Heaven
Have I oft wondered were my father there
So gently tender and so fondly proud—
Blest by the presence of that sister drowned
When I myself was saved.


### GIOVANNI.

How came it so ?


### GIACOMO.

I know not.   Many an hour have I spent

Slow wandering 'mongst the tombs of San
    Michele
There searching for the name of him I called
My father, tho' his face would seem to me
So like to all Venetians I would fain
Have met him in the glare of noonday sun
And turned me from him.

### GIOVANNI.

                His death was not
Unlike thy sister's, then?

### GIACOMO.

                Methinks the same.
'T was thus: Giudecca held in bondage knights
And factious nobles whose allegiance blent
With such stern hatred for Venetian powers,
That Venice was to them a state forbidden.
My father, one such night, though bolder far
Than such as choked with hearts up in their
    throats,
Did not consent to stay and languish there
But in a boat disguis'd did strive to reach
Fair Venice.  As we sped with muffled oar,
A sentinel stove in our bow; we 'gan to sink,

Paola cried, and clung to me for help:—
I swam with boyish strength ; there on my back
I bore the life that unto me was all in all ;
Then suddenly her weight slipped off, and I
In agony swam toward the shore,—was saved,
But saved an orphan, mourning at the age
When children know no woe.   I roamed about
An heir to that enforced seclusion whence
My parents strove to 'scape, but instead
Did win that freedom which cold death doth
      grant.

(GIACOMO *turns and addresses* PAOLA.)

A year or more agone. I saw thy face
And formed of it the image of my hope,
A hope that from a nameless youth's warm
      heart
Hath filled his brain with dreams of lighter life.
Before King Carnival blew his jolly horn
I followed thee to this fair palace gate.
In this sped year I've pauséd many times :
Methought I was some Servite friar lean
Who from Calle Fallier descended oft
To gather from the poor such small stipend
Of bread or wood as he was wont to beg
Against the winter's cold and gnawing want,

Thy face has blest so many hours of dread
And pain and misery that I do crave
Thy pardon if thou dost not upon me look
With favor.

        So yestere'en did come when I
In seemly distance lounged behind thy boat
Unwittingly waiting for the grave mishap
That plunged thee into water ne'er so warm
But that the summer's sun might make it
      warm ;
You call me brave, 't was but a natural course.
I will not try your patience any more,
But unto this good man I would remind
That when true love outweighs the love of
      gold,
And honest love will grant an honest name
The weight of true nobility, I will crave
The hand of her who is my saint.   My tale
Doth end.

### GIOVANNI.

      Thy tale is not half told.   'T is well
I now must grant my praise ; and, too, I grant
At once this saint who evermore shalt bless
And sweeten life for thee.

### GIACOMO.

My bride!

### GIOVANNI.

Not so!
Thy sister that was drowned has come to life,
And I your Father am, and this your Mother;—
Death took us not, it was for you we mourned.

### ROSALBA.

My son?

### GIOVANNI.

Thy son!

### ROSALBA.

It seemeth but a dream!

### GIACOMO.

No bride? Alas! I am so stupefied
I know not whence this blow has fallen. Thou
My sister? Thou, my Mother? Thou,—O
    Mother,
Thus let me on thy tender bosom rest.

No bride?   Alas, it is a grief so grave;
And yet, all life begins anew, and thou
Dear Sister, to me shalt be so dear that I
Will call thee sweetheart mine.   So kiss I thee.
No bride?   Alas, I understand it not.

PAOLA.

That bride must in thy Sister be forgot.

February, 1892.

# Giacomo: A Venetian Tale

By
WILLIAM
CUSHING
BAMBURGH

NEW YORK CITY:
PRIVATELY PRINTED FOR THE AUTHOR
MDCCCXCII